The Birthday Swap

written and illustrated by LORETTA LOPEZ

LEE & LOW BOOKS Inc. • NEW YORK

In memory of Jax

With deepest thanks to Liz and Christy, for your faith, support, and endless patience...

For Armida, who really did swap. Thanks, Sis! XO—L.L.

Text and Illustrations copyright © 1997 by Loretta Lopez
LEE & LOW BOOKS Inc., 95 Madison Avenue, New York, NY 10016
leeandlow.com

Manufactured in China by RR Donnelley

Book Design by Christy Hale
Book Production by The Kids at Our House

The text is set in Myriad Tilt
The illustrations are rendered in gouache and colored pencil on watercolor paper
Printed on paper from responsible sources

(HC) 10 9 8 7 6 5
(PB) 25 24 23 22 21 20
First Edition

Library of Congress Cataloging-in-Publication Data
Lopez, Loretta.
The birthday swap/[text and illustrations] by Loretta Lopez.—1st ed.
p.   cm.
Summary: A five-year-old Mexican American girl who will not be six until December has a great deal to celebrate when her sister swaps birthdays with her in the summer.
ISBN 978-1-880000-47-2 (hardcover)   ISBN 978-1-88-0000-89-2 (paperback)
[1. Birthdays—Fiction. 2. Mexican Americans—Fiction. 3. Sisters—Fiction.] I. Title.
PZ7.L87636Bi 1997   [E]—dc20   96-24136   CIP AC

FSC
www.fsc.org
MIX
Paper from
responsible sources
FSC® C144853

Glossary

Feliz Cumpleaños (feh-LEEZ coom-plee-AHN-yos): Happy Birthday

mercado (mehr-KAH-doh): market

Mija (MEE-ha): my daughter

tia (TEE-ah): aunt

tio (TEE-oh): uncle

My name is Lori. I'm the youngest one in my family. I grew up in a town near the border between the United States and Mexico. Half my relatives live in Mexico, and half of them live here. This is a picture that my dad took at a party in Mexico, the year I turned six. My brothers, Ed and Beto, and my sister Cookie were teenagers then. That was the year of the best birthday party ever, and this is the story of how it happened.

It was a Saturday morning in summer, the day before my sister Cookie's birthday. Every year we celebrated Cookie's birthday with a big family reunion and cookout at Tio Daniel's house in Mexico. This year I wanted to get Cookie my own present, instead of just adding my name to whatever my parents were giving her. But I couldn't come up with an idea for a gift.

When I told my mom, she smiled and said, "She doesn't expect you to give her a present, Mija."

"But I want to," I said. "Only she's so much older than me, it's hard to find the right thing."

"Well, think," Dad said. "What would you want?"

I thought about it. My birthday wasn't till December.

"A horse!" I shouted. My parents gave each other a look.

"Too big for the backyard," Dad pointed out. "What else?"

"A kitten!"

Mom shook her head. "Cookie's allergic to cats. And so am I."

"Try again," Dad said hopefully. "What would you want, more than anything in the world?"

It hit me—the perfect gift! "A puppy!"

Dad smiled, but Mom looked stern. "A puppy is a big responsibility. Cookie's starting her senior year this fall. She won't have time to care for a pet."

"I could help," I offered.

"Tell you what," Mom said. "Why don't you come with me on my errands? Maybe you'll find something, okay?"

Mom and I drove over the bridge and across the border. Our first stop was Tia Sabina's house. I loved visiting Tia Sabina. She was a baker, and her house smelled good, like cakes and melted candle wax.

Tia Sabina was finishing up a huge cake. She kissed me and patted my cheek with her soft, sugary hands.

"How are you today?" she asked.

"Not so good, Tia. I don't have a present for Cookie."

"Oh, don't worry about that," Tia said. "Maybe you'll think of something while your mother and I discuss cake business." Mom and Tia went into the kitchen. I wandered around and looked at cake decorations. But I still didn't come up with any great ideas.

Our next stop was the Mercado. The market in Mexico was totally different from the supermarket at home. For one thing, the Mercado was always noisy and crowded, with shoppers and vendors and musicians. There was even a special section for live animals, with chickens, ducks, parakeets, and even donkeys for sale!

Mom headed straight for the fruit and vegetable stands. I saw a huge bin of shiny red tomatoes. *Cookie loves tomatoes,* I thought. I picked one up. Somehow, a tomato just wasn't special enough.

"What do you think?" I asked a kitten at my feet.

"Neooo," it meowed in a tiny voice.

I put the tomato back and walked with Mom to the curio shop, where all the toys and trinkets for tourists were sold. Great things! Ceramic piggy banks, marionettes, maracas, glass animals, and big sombreros with fancy needlework and sequins. I could have wandered around in that shop for hours, but I realized after a few minutes that nothing was quite right for Cookie.

n our way back to the car, we passed the piñatas.

"Just a second," Mom said, and then began talking quietly with the piñata maker in Spanish. I walked around and made friends. My favorite was the donkey.

"Mom, how about this?" I asked.

"I think Cookie's too old for a piñata, don't you?" she said, taking my hand as we walked back to the car. "Don't worry, it'll be okay."

The next morning I was the last one up. Our house was crazy—everybody was running around getting ready for the big party. Mom had even made me a new dress to wear to church. She fixed my hair with blue satin ribbons.

"Boy, I sure am going fancy to church today," I said.

My mother just raised her eyebrows and smiled. Grownups!

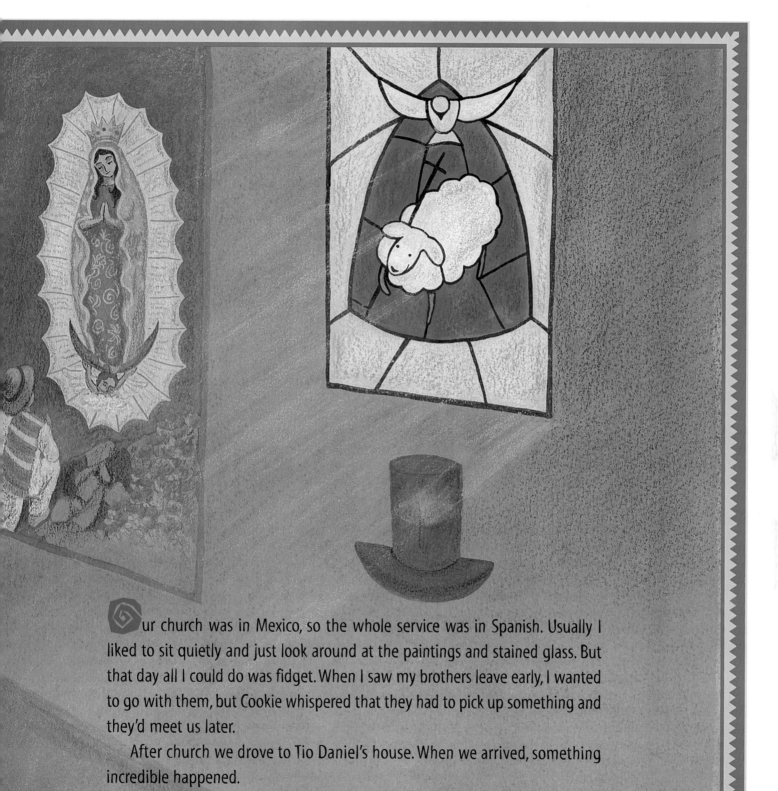

ur church was in Mexico, so the whole service was in Spanish. Usually I liked to sit quietly and just look around at the paintings and stained glass. But that day all I could do was fidget. When I saw my brothers leave early, I wanted to go with them, but Cookie whispered that they had to pick up something and they'd meet us later.

After church we drove to Tio Daniel's house. When we arrived, something incredible happened.

"**S**urprise! Happy Birthday, Lori! Feliz Cumpleaños!"

Everyone was there. My grandparents, aunts, and uncles. All my friends. Our neighbors. My cousins from both sides of the border. Everyone!

"But," I said, "it's not my birthday."

"Well, it's like this," Cookie explained. "Because my birthday is in the summer,

I always get a big party. But since your birthday is in winter when it's too cold, you never get one. So this year I thought I'd swap with you. After all, I'm getting a little old for this.

"So," Cookie smiled. "Happy Birthday!"

I was so surprised. I hugged my sister and ran to join the party.

What a day! We swam in Tio Daniel's pool, we played tag, and we ate! There was so much food, I can't even remember it all. In the center of the table was the beautiful cake I'd seen at Tia Sabina's the day before, with seven candles on it—six plus one for good luck.

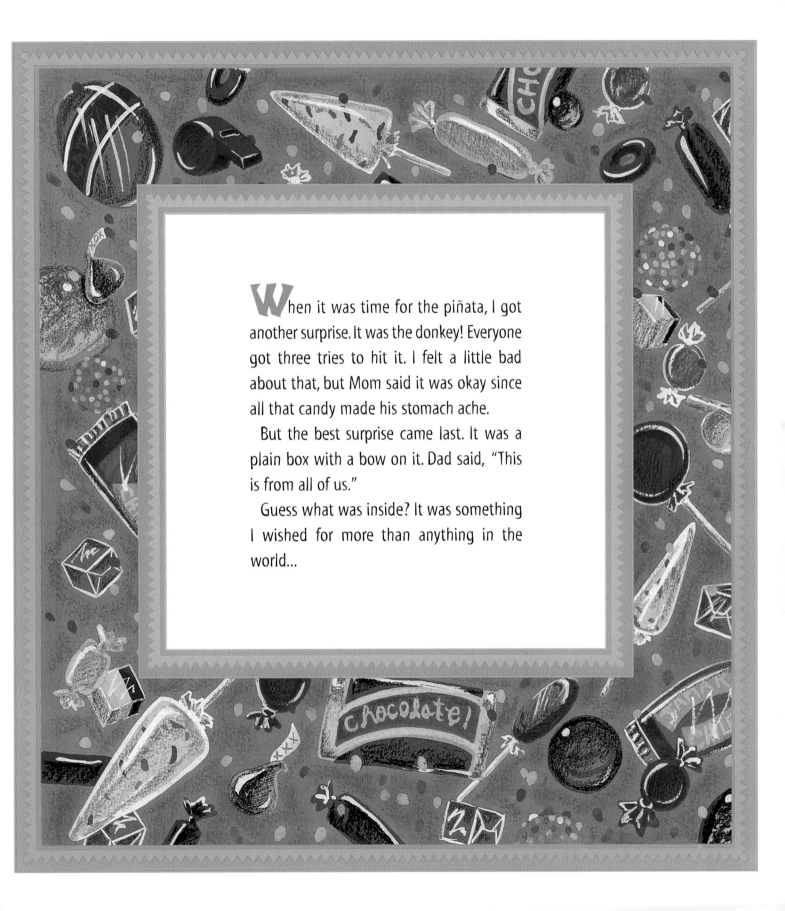

When it was time for the piñata, I got another surprise. It was the donkey! Everyone got three tries to hit it. I felt a little bad about that, but Mom said it was okay since all that candy made his stomach ache.

But the best surprise came last. It was a plain box with a bow on it. Dad said, "This is from all of us."

Guess what was inside? It was something I wished for more than anything in the world...

A puppy!
I picked her up. She wiggled
and licked my face.
"Her name is Spicy!" I said,
and everyone clapped.

I played with Spicy and had some more cake and ice cream. The sun started to set. A mariachi band arrived, and soon everyone was dancing. After a while, all the kids got tired and started to fall asleep on the grass.

I tried to stay awake, but I guess I fell asleep, too.

Cookie said the party got really loud. I didn't wake up, though. Mom said that when it was over, Dad carried me to the car. The next thing I knew I was home in bed.

So that's what happened. My sister swapped my birthday for hers, and I think that's one of the nicest things anybody could ever do.

Good night!